With thanks and admiration to all of Peter Blake's whanau
— D.H.

For my grandpa, Michael Morris
— P.M.

PUFFIN

UK | USA | Canada | Ireland | Australia
India | New Zealand | South Africa | China

Puffin is an imprint of the Penguin Random House
group of companies, whose addresses can be found at
global.penguinrandomhouse.com.

First published by Penguin Random House New Zealand, 2018

10 9 8 7 6 5 4 3 2

Text © David Hill, 2018
Illustrations © Phoebe Morris, 2018

Design by Cat Taylor © Penguin Random House New Zealand
Prepress by Image Centre Group
Printed and bound in China by Donnelley Asia

A catalogue record for this book is available from the National
Library of New Zealand.

ISBN 978-0-14-377165-4

The assistance of Creative New Zealand towards the production
of this book is gratefully acknowledged by the publisher.

penguin.co.nz

HERO
OF THE
SEA

Sir Peter Blake's Mighty Ocean Quests

David Hill

Illustrated by
Phoebe Morris

PUFFIN

He was over 1.9 metres tall, with fair hair and a loud happy laugh.

He was one of the world's greatest yachtsmen, and he worked to help protect the environment.

His name was Peter Blake.

Peter was born in 1948, on Auckland's North Shore.

By the time he was eight, Peter was racing.

The Blakes' back garden sloped down to the Waitemata Harbour. Peter and his younger brother Tony explored nearby bays in a dinghy.

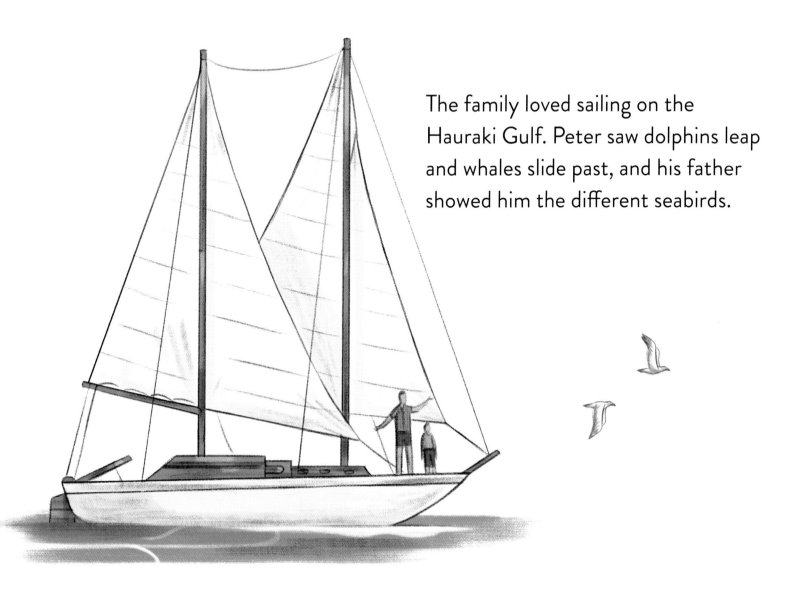

The family loved sailing on the Hauraki Gulf. Peter saw dolphins leap and whales slide past, and his father showed him the different seabirds.

Peter became one of Auckland's best teenage sailors, strong and careful. He learned to navigate by watching the stars reflected in a bucket of water.

Inside a shed on the lawn, Peter built a yacht. He named it *Bandit*.
Then he and Tony tore over the waves, bright sails flying.

Even before he left school, word had
spread about this tall, blond young man.
Skippers of big yachts asked him to join
their crews. A life of sailing lay ahead.

In 1973, Peter sailed in the first ever Whitbread Round the World Race.

Their yacht leaked — one of the crew had to sleep under an umbrella. Then, in giant waves, the boat started to break apart. They had to stop racing while they made repairs.

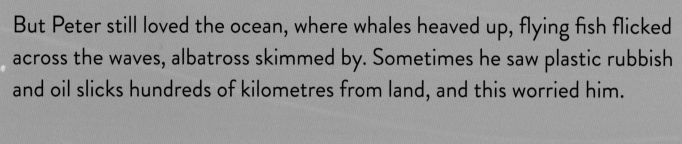

But Peter still loved the ocean, where whales heaved up, flying fish flicked across the waves, albatross skimmed by. Sometimes he saw plastic rubbish and oil slicks hundreds of kilometres from land, and this worried him.

In 1977, he crewed on his second Whitbread race.

This time, a sailor fell overboard. He was only found because a flock of albatross circled him. Ocean life was important in many ways.

When the race brought Peter to England, he met a young woman who also loved adventures. Her name was Pippa. Peter proposed to her in a yacht harbour.

Pippa was a good sailor. And an artist. And a planner. She and the team helped organise Peter's long voyages.

Ocean life was also exciting in many ways. There were more races, fast and dangerous.

In the next Whitbread, the mast of Peter's *Ceramco* broke. But Peter's crew knew they had a great skipper. They liked the way he ended every order with "Please".

In the Whitbread after that, Peter's *Lion* bumped into whales and a 1000-kilogram sunfish.

Peter wanted young people to have the chance to enjoy sailing. He travelled around New Zealand raising money for a training ship. That ship became known as the *Spirit of New Zealand*.

Pippa and Peter's children, Sarah-Jane and James, often sailed with them on their trips. Pippa and Peter gave the children tiny sets of yachting gear. The New Zealanders in the crew taught them to say "Chill out".

Peter's *Steinlager 2* won the 1989 Whitbread, though the wind sometimes blew them along so hard they didn't dare put up any sails.

Of course they won. Peter had a secret weapon: his socks.

Before every big race, Pippa would give him a pair. These ones were bright green. A whale swam right up to *Steinlager 2*, and stared. Maybe it liked Peter's socks?

His next pair became famous.

The USA had held the America's Cup yachting trophy for over 130 years. Peter was invited to help organise the 1995 New Zealand challenge.

For this race, Pippa had given him a red pair of socks. So, to raise money for the America's Cup challenge, red socks were sold all across New Zealand.

The Prime Minister and thousands of others wore them. So did the elephant at Auckland Zoo. People flew red socks from car aerials. A giant pair hung from Parliament Buildings in Wellington.

New Zealand's yacht *Black Magic*, with Peter and his red socks on board, won every race against the America's Cup holders. It went like "a black torpedo".

When Peter and the team arrived home, another huge pair of red socks dangled from a hot air balloon at Auckland Airport.

Peter became Sir Peter Blake, for services to yachting.
(He was in the bath when he heard.)

Peter had always loved the bird and animal life of the ocean. "Remember," he wrote, "This is THE most beautiful world, and it's the ONLY one we've got."

Peter bought a boat that he called *Seamaster*. He and some friends planned to take it to the Antarctic, the Amazon River, coral reefs, and other places where water, trees and wildlife were in danger. They would make TV documentaries about what they found.

In November 2000, *Seamaster* sailed south. First they arrived at the bottom of South America, where the Blake family watched great chunks of glaciers crashing into the sea.

Then *Seamaster* sailed on to Antarctica, past ice where thousands of penguins and seals lived. Humpback whales, as long as a cricket pitch, swam around them.

It was so cold that sails froze solid, but when the crew measured the ice, they found that climate change was melting it much faster than normal.

Next, *Seamaster* turned north, towards a very different place. It headed for the tropical jungle of the Amazon, our planet's biggest river. Peter wanted to see how much forest was being cut down, and the damage to plants and animals.

Pippa was an expedition artist, and she drew riverbanks, jungle and water. They saw piranha, pink dolphins, alligators, turtles.

Peter wrote that "one breath out of every five we take comes from Amazon trees". But they saw that enormous sections of forest had been felled to make new farms. Forest people had to leave their homes. The Amazon water was getting more and more polluted. So many fish were being taken that some villages didn't have enough to eat.

Then, one night on their return downriver, *Seamaster* lay at anchor. Eight pirates with guns rushed on board. When Peter tried to make them leave, he was shot and killed.

All across the world, people mourned.

"We want to make a difference," Peter had written.

He has.

Today, the Sir Peter Blake Trust helps young New Zealanders learn about the environment and become leaders. *Black Magic* stands inside the Auckland Maritime Museum. Schools hold Red Sock Days to raise funds for Sir Peter's Trust. And many of New Zealand's top sailors say how lucky they are to have sailed with Sir Peter Blake.

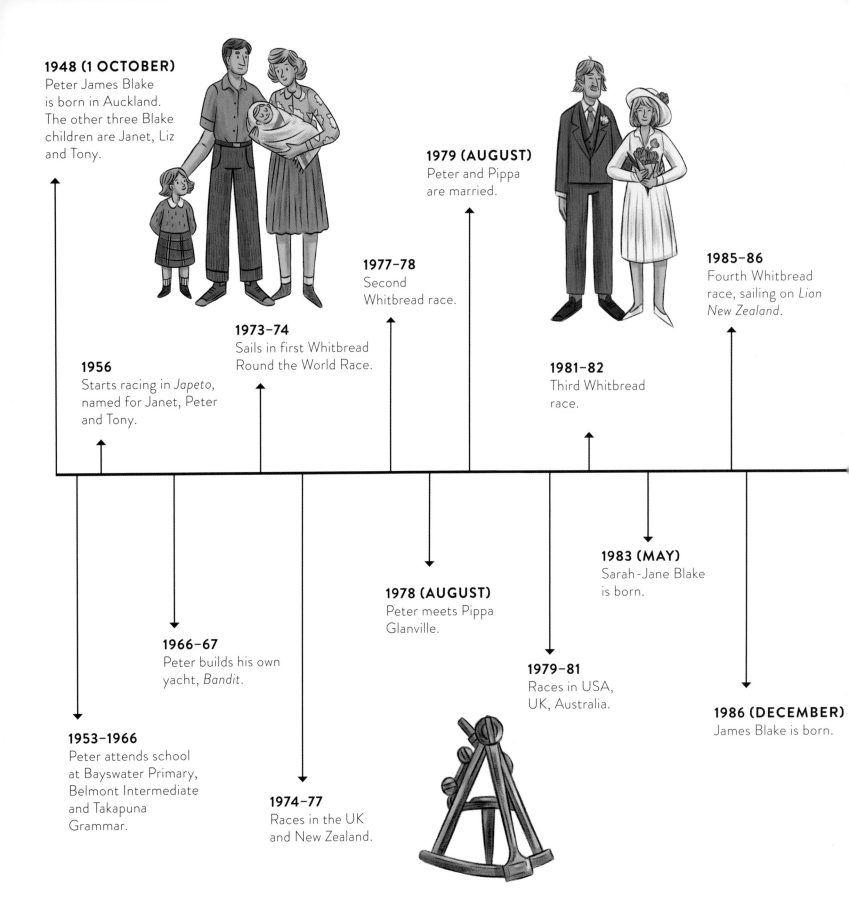

1948 (1 OCTOBER)
Peter James Blake is born in Auckland. The other three Blake children are Janet, Liz and Tony.

1956
Starts racing in *Japeto*, named for Janet, Peter and Tony.

1953–1966
Peter attends school at Bayswater Primary, Belmont Intermediate and Takapuna Grammar.

1966–67
Peter builds his own yacht, *Bandit*.

1973–74
Sails in first Whitbread Round the World Race.

1974–77
Races in the UK and New Zealand.

1977–78
Second Whitbread race.

1978 (AUGUST)
Peter meets Pippa Glanville.

1979 (AUGUST)
Peter and Pippa are married.

1979–81
Races in USA, UK, Australia.

1981–82
Third Whitbread race.

1983 (MAY)
Sarah-Jane Blake is born.

1985–86
Fourth Whitbread race, sailing on *Lion New Zealand*.

1986 (DECEMBER)
James Blake is born.

1989–90
Wins the fifth Whitbread race on *Steinlager 2*.

1991–92
Peter is appointed manager of New Zealand's America's Cup challenge.

1993–94
Sails in Jules Verne races. Winner of second race on *ENZA*.

1995
Heads New Zealand's America's Cup challenge. *NZL 32 Black Magic* wins every race.

1995
Knighted to become Sir Peter Blake.

2000
NZL 60 Black Magic defends the America's Cup, winning every race.

2000 (NOVEMBER)–2001 (MARCH)
Now a UN Special Envoy for the Environment, Peter sails to South America and Antarctica on *Seamaster*.

2001 (SEPTEMBER–DECEMBER)
Peter sails up the Amazon River on *Seamaster*.

2001 (6 DECEMBER)
Peter is killed when pirates attack *Seamaster*.

2004
The Sir Peter Blake Trust is established.

2013
Peter's yacht *Bandit* is found in a Northland shed and restored.

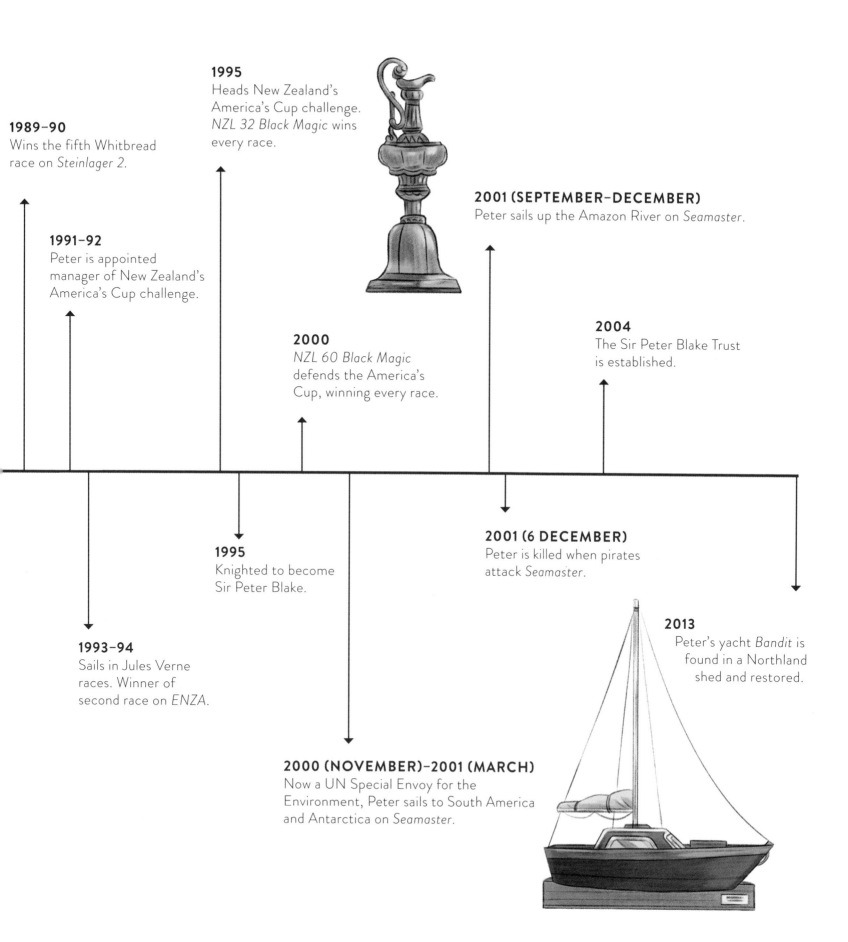

Pippa is now a successful artist.

Sarah-Jane is also an artist, and an ocean adventurer.

James makes films about the environment and expeditions.

The Sir Peter Blake Trust is based in Auckland. It educates young New Zealanders about challenges like climate change and plastics in the ocean, and gives them the opportunity to travel on expeditions to some of New Zealand's most unique and special places, like the Kermadec and Sub-Antarctic islands. It helps students, scientists, teachers and other people who want to make our world a better place — just like Peter did.